An I Can Read Book™

Adventures of Harold and His Friends

INCLUDING:

The Giant Garden

Animals, Animals, Animals

The Birthday Present

Harold Finds a Friend

BARNES & NOBLE

NEW YORK

Barnes and Noble Publishing, Inc.
122 Fifth Avenue
New York, NY 10011

ISBN: 0-7607-7109-X

Manufactured in China

08 09 MCH 10 9 8 7 6

HAROLD and the PURPLE CRAYON™

The Giant Garden

Adaptation by Valerie Garfield
Based on a teleplay by Don Gillies
Illustrations by Kevin Murawski

Harold was tucked in bed

but he couldn't fall asleep.

He was watching a little
ladybug on his windowsill.

"What is it like to be as small

as a ladybug?" Harold wondered.

He picked up his purple crayon

and drew a path.

Then he stepped onto it.

Ladybugs live in gardens,

so Harold drew a packet of seeds.

The plants grew,

and grew, and grew.

Harold felt tiny.

He felt as tiny as a ladybug!

9

Harold jumped from one leaf to
the other.

Then he came to a big pond.

Harold leaped onto a lily pad.

Then he drew an oar and . . .

. . . paddled right into a frog!

The frog looked very big.

The frog looked very hungry!

Harold drew a huge gumdrop.

He threw it to the frog.

Slurp! The frog lapped it up!

Harold paddled away very quickly.

Harold climbed over a big leaf

and saw another ladybug!

They had a tea party.

They played hide-and-seek.

How would Harold find the

ladybug?

Harold found his ladybug friend.

Oh, no!

Harold's new friend was stuck

in a spiderweb.

Harold jumped into the web.

It was sticky!

Harold drew a pair of scissors.

Snip, snip!

The ladybug was free!

The ladybug was so happy
to be free that she invited Harold
to meet her family.

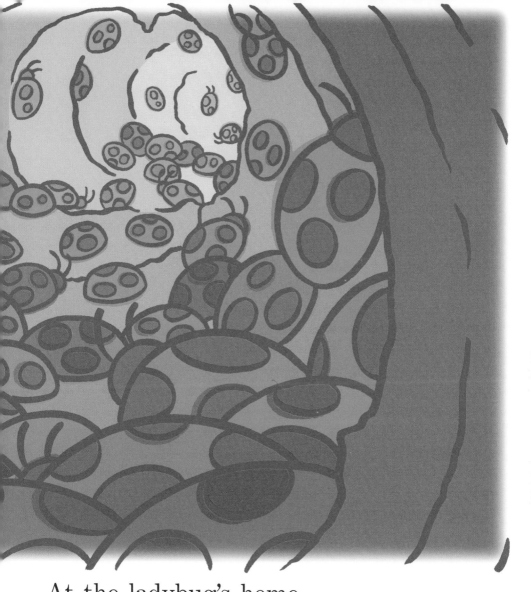

At the ladybug's home,

Harold couldn't believe his eyes.

He had never seen so many ladybugs!

He had never seen so many spots!

Harold lost his ladybug friend,

but he met an ant.

The ant was looking for food

to bring to the queen ant.

Harold helped the ant look.

They found a picnic lunch.

The ant saw some bananas

leaning against a bowl of fruit.

Harold drew a rope,

and lassoed a banana.

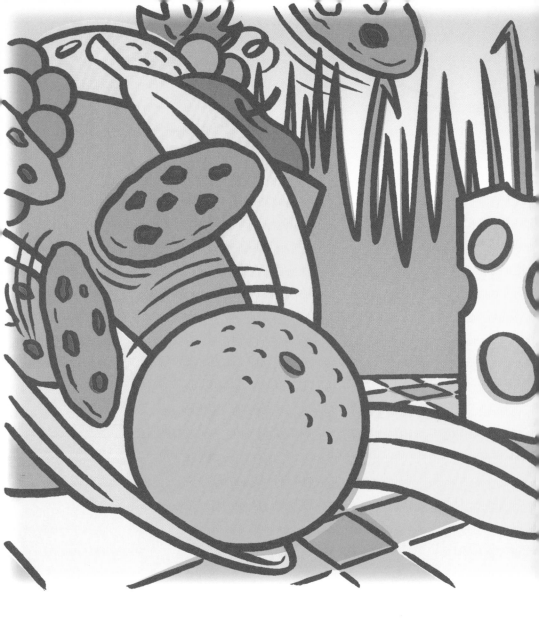

Harold tugged and the banana fell.

An orange rolled down onto

a plate of cookies.

It sent the cookies flying!
Harold and the ant ran
out of the way.

The cookies broke on the ground.

Harold and the ant each picked
up a piece of cookie to carry to
the queen ant.

The queen was so happy!

She made Harold her king.

Harold drew a crown and sat

beside the queen.

The queen was very nice to Harold.

She offered him some of her food.

Harold knew never to eat something

that had fallen on the floor.

Harold began to feel sleepy.

He wanted to be in his own bed.

So he set off to find the moon.

Harold found the moon.

He drew his bedroom window

around it.

He crawled into his cozy bed.

His purple crayon

dropped to the floor.

And Harold dropped off to sleep.

Harold wonders what it's like to be an elephant!

HAROLD and the PURPLE CRAYON™

Animals, Animals, Animals!

Adaptation by Liza Baker
Based on a teleplay by Don Gillies
Illustrations by Andy Chiang,
Jose Lopez, and Kevin Murawski

Harold couldn't sleep,

so he took out his stuffed animals.

Harold thought about

how much fun animals have.

What animal would I like to be?

he wondered.

Harold wanted to find out
more about animals.

He picked up his purple crayon

and set off on an adventure.

Harold thought,

I would like to be big and strong.

He took his crayon and drew an elephant.

The elephant dipped its trunk

into a bucket of water.

Then he sprayed water all around.

It looked like fun.

So Harold drew a hose.

But the hose was very wiggly.

Harold accidentally sprayed the elephant.

The elephant got all wet.

Harold tried to apologize,

but the elephant walked away.

I would like to take long trips,

thought Harold.

So he drew a camel.

Then Harold drew a large backpack
full of food and water.
Together, Harold and the camel
set off through the desert.

As Harold walked,

the backpack felt very heavy.

Harold was tired.

The sun was hot.

He drew a lake and a palm tree.

As Harold rested,

a herd of cheetahs ran by.

I would like to move really fast,

thought Harold.

Harold drew a pair of roller skates

and raced after the cheetahs.

Racing with the cheetahs was fun,

but soon Harold was hot again.

He wanted to go somewhere cool.

Harold took his crayon

and drew a line up to the sky.

He found himself on

top of a snow-covered hill.

Harold met a group of penguins.
They were sliding one by one on
their bellies down the slope.

I would like to slide down a snowy hill, thought Harold.

So he drew a sled.

Many penguins jumped on with Harold.

Soon the sled was full of penguins.

The sled sped down the hill.

With a crash, Harold and the
penguins landed in the snow.

Harold was covered with snow.

He was cold.

He drew a big sun in the sky.

Harold was warm again.

He drew a jungle.

Monkeys played on vines.

I would like to swing, thought Harold.

He reached up and grabbed a vine.

Soon he was swinging back and forth

just like the monkeys.

Living the life of the animals

had been fun.

But Harold liked being himself best.

Harold took his purple crayon and
drew his bedroom window.

Back in his room,

Harold pulled up his covers.

As he hugged Lilac in his arms,

his purple crayon dropped to the floor,

and Harold dropped off to sleep.

What will Harold get his mother for her birthday?

HAROLD and the PURPLE CRAYON™

The Birthday Present

Adaptation by Valerie Garfield
Illustrations by Kevin Murawski

Harold couldn't sleep.

His mother's birthday

was the next day.

Harold didn't know what to give her.

He wanted to find the perfect
birthday present.

Harold didn't think he could find it

in his bedroom,

so he picked up his purple crayon

and set off on an adventure.

Harold decided to go for a walk.

He drew a path

and started on his way.

Harold drew a tree.

It was such a nice tree

that he drew one more,

and one more,

and one more.

Soon there was a forest.

Harold walked under the trees.

They were so tall

they stretched up to the sky.

Harold didn't know which way to go.

Harold climbed to the top of a tree

and looked in every direction.

But he couldn't find his way out.

Harold knew what to do.

He drew a bird

and flew to the edge of the forest

on the bird's back.

Harold came to a stream.

On the other side,

he saw a big field of flowers.

Harold drew a bridge

and crossed over to the other side.

Now the sun was high.

It was very hot, and the flowers

were sleepy and droopy.

The flowers needed water.

Harold reached as high as he could

and drew a big rain cloud in the sky.

The cloud blocked out the sun.

Drip! Drip! Drip!

Rain came down from the cloud.

Harold drew an even bigger cloud.

Drip, drop! Drip, drop!

The rain poured down on Harold's head.

Harold drew an umbrella

as quickly as he could.

The flowers weren't thirsty anymore,

but they still looked droopy.

Flowers need water and . . .

Sun!

Harold drew a gust of wind

to blow the clouds away.

The sun sent bright rays

of sunshine down to the flowers.

One by one they lifted their heads

to the warm light.

Harold looked at the pretty flowers.

His mother loved flowers.

Flowers would be

the perfect birthday present!

Now Harold had another problem.
He couldn't take the whole field
home with him.

Harold had an idea.

He thought of the perfect gift.

But it was at home.

How could he get back?

Then Harold remembered

that he could always see the moon

from his bedroom window.

Harold drew his bedroom window
around the moon.

Back in his bedroom, Harold realized
that the perfect gift for his mother
had been right at his fingertips
the whole time!

Harold would give his mother a flower.

He knew she would love it.

She could keep this flower forever,

and it wouldn't need water or sunlight.

When Harold finished the flower,

he left the picture where his

mother would see it.

Then he climbed into bed.

Then Harold dropped off to sleep.

And Harold's purple crayon

dropped to the floor.

Harold and Lilac
have fun together.

HAROLD and the PURPLE CRAYON™

Harold Finds a Friend

Text by Liza Baker
Based on a teleplay by Carin Greenberg Baker
Illustrations by Kevin Murawski

Harold couldn't sleep.

He wanted to play, but he had

no one to play with.

He decided to play

with his stuffed dog, Lilac.

He threw a rubber ball

across the room.

Lilac didn't chase the ball.

Lilac didn't bring the ball back.

She couldn't.

Lilac was just a stuffed animal.

Harold wanted a real dog,

so he picked up his purple crayon

and set off on an adventure.

Harold drew a path and
started on his way.

He drew a rubber ball.

It was perfect for playing catch.

Harold threw the ball,

and it bounced away.

Lilac caught the ball.

She brought it to Harold.

Harold tossed the ball again.

Once more, Lilac chased after it.

At last, Harold had a dog who

liked to play catch.

Lilac was good at tricks, too.

A dog who does tricks deserves a
reward, so Harold drew a big box
of dog biscuits.

After each trick,

Harold gave Lilac a biscuit.

"Good dog," he said.

But Lilac was impatient.

She jumped onto Harold's lap.

She grabbed the box of biscuits

and started digging a hole.

Lilac was trying to bury the box.
She kicked dirt into the air and
covered Harold from head to toe.

Harold told Lilac to stop.

She looked sad.

Her feelings were hurt.

Lilac ran away.

Harold was alone again.

He decided to wait for Lilac

to come back.

He was tired, so he drew a chair.

Harold waited for a long time.

He grew bored.

Then he had an idea.

He'd draw a new friend.

Harold drew a large round bowl.

Then he drew a plump goldfish.

But the fish didn't want to play.

It just swam in circles.

So Harold drew a big dog.

The dog sat down, rolled over,

and fell asleep.

A sleeping dog isn't any fun,

thought Harold.

Harold drew a very peppy dog.

Harold drew a ball and threw it.

But instead of bringing it back,

the dog played with the ball

all by itself.

This dog was no fun.

Lilac was a good friend,

even when she misbehaved.

Harold had to find her,

so he drew a lighthouse.

He climbed the stairs

to the highest point.

He followed the path of the light

and looked in every direction.

Finally, he spotted Lilac.

Harold rushed to Lilac.

Harold patted her happily.

Lilac wagged her tail.

She was happy, too.

Harold drew another ball.

He threw it for Lilac again and again

until they were tired.

Harold and Lilac rested.

Then it was time to go home.

Harold reached up and drew his

bedroom window around the moon.

Harold was back in his bedroom.

Harold slipped into bed.

He was happy to be home with

his good friend Lilac.

As he curled up with Lilac,
Harold's purple crayon dropped
to the floor.
And he dropped off to sleep.